For Amber

T.H.

For Becky

D.W.

HAMISH HAMILTON LTD

Published by the Penguin Group
27 Wrights Lane, London w8 5tz, England
Penguin Books USA Inc., 375 Hudson Street, New York, New York 10014, USA
Penguin Books Australia Ltd, Ringwood, Victoria, Australia
Penguin Books Canada Ltd, 10 Alcorn Avenue, Toronto, Ontario, Canada m4v 3b2
Penguin Books (NZ) Ltd, 182–190 Wairau Road, Auckland 10, New Zealand

Penguin Books Ltd, Registered Offices: Harmondsworth, Middlesex, England

First published in Great Britain 1991 by Hamish Hamilton Ltd

Text copyright © 1991 by David Wood
Illustrations copyright © 1991 by Tony Husband

1 3 5 7 9 10 8 6 4 2

A CIP catalogue record for this book is available from the British Library

isbn 0-241-13137-5

Set in 15pt Baskerville by Rowland Phototypesetting Ltd
Bury St Edmunds, Suffolk
Printed in Great Britain by
BPCC Hazell Books Ltd, Member of BPCC Ltd, Aylesbury, Bucks.

Chapter 1

"EAT UP, BECKY," said Mrs Bear.
"You'll be late for school."

"Oh, Mum," groaned Becky Bear.
"The cartoon's on."

"You can't watch television and eat
your breakfast at the same time,"
sighed her mother.

"I can, Mum, look," replied Becky,
taking a big bite of toast and honey.

Ben Bear, Becky's little brother, was
happily building a mountain with his
soggy cornflakes.

"Eat them, Ben, don't play with them," growled Mr Bear, then went back to his newspaper.

Ben's face crumpled and he started to sob.

"Quiet, Ben," said Mrs Bear. "I want to listen." She turned up the volume on the television. The cartoon had finished and the news was starting.

Becky grinned. "You can't watch television and eat your breakfast at the same time, Mum," she called.

"Don't be cheeky, Becky," replied her mother. "Anyway, I've finished my breakfast. You watch the news. You might learn something."

Becky usually found the news boring. But she watched anyway. Onto the screen flashed the familiar face of a dog.

"Good morning, good morning," he barked. "This is Newshound with the latest update. Three more human tower blocks have been knocked down to make way for a young animals' adventure forest and play area. Many humans who had refused to evacuate the buildings were finally forced out of their homes."

Onto the screen came pictures of hundreds of human beings carrying a few hastily packed belongings as they fled screaming from the advancing bulldozers. Becky found it frightening, but kept watching. The face of Newshound returned. "Many child humans," he announced, "got trampled in the stampede. And now the latest pop video from the Funky Monkies!"

As the music started, Mrs Bear

turned the volume down. "I don't know what the world's coming to," she sighed.

"Oh, Mum," protested Becky. "The Funky Monkies aren't that bad."

"Not the Funky Monkies, silly. That news report. How could we animals be so cruel to those defenceless humans? Open wide, Ben." Ben reluctantly opened his mouth and Mrs Bear popped in a spoonful of cereal.

Becky thought for a moment. "What will happen to them all, Mum?" she asked quietly.

"Those humans? Well, some may find somewhere else to live," replied her mother. "But lots won't make it."

"You mean they'll die?"

"Of course. The more we take away their natural habitat, all those housing estates and blocks of flats we keep destroying, the less chance of survival the humans have. Before long they'll become extinct."

"*I* want a drink!" cried Ben.

"Please," snapped Mrs Bear.

"Please," whispered Ben.

"Why do we do it?" asked Becky.

"It's called progress," grunted her father, putting down his newspaper and buttering a piece of toast. "Animals need adventure forests to play in and there aren't enough of them. So the human homes have to go."

"But it's not fair," said Becky. "I wouldn't treat Norman like that." She got up and gently stroked the human curled up asleep in his basket under the television.

"That's different," smiled her father. "Norman's our pet-human."

"I love Norman," gurgled Ben.

"Of course you do, darling," said Mrs Bear. "We all love Norman." She gazed fondly down at Norman, who, hearing his name, opened one trusting eye. "Hallo, Norman! Who's a good boy?" she cooed. "Is Norman hungry? Is Norman a hungry human? Does he want his brekky? Does he? Good boy!"

"I'll get it," smiled Becky, as Norman jumped eagerly from his basket. She opened a tin of human-food and emptied it into his bowl. Norman gratefully tucked in.

"Of course," said Mr Bear, "not all animals love their pet-humans as much as we do. Look how many animals are given baby pet-humans as birthday presents or Christmas presents, play with them for a few days, and then decide they don't want them after all." He pointed to his newspaper. "There's a story today of two baby pet-humans tied in a bag by their owners and thrown in the river. If a passing cow hadn't spotted them and saved them, they would have drowned. The cow's looking for good homes for them."

"Good for her," said Mrs Bear. "Now come on, Becky. School."

Chapter 2

BECKY BEAR WAS thoughtful as she walked to school. The street was busy as animals noisily hurried to work in their animobiles or on animobuses, but Becky hardly noticed them. She forgot to pay her usual visit to Mrs Fox's sweet shop to buy something tasty for morning break. Her head was full of those television pictures of unhappy humans forced to leave their homes. Just think how we would feel, she thought, Mum and Dad and Ben and me, if we had nowhere to live.

Suddenly her thoughts were interrupted by a disturbance across the street. A family of human refugees, tired and hungry, had taken shelter in a shop doorway.

Two Police Dogs, each holding a sniffer-human on a lead, were forcing the humans to stand up.

"Move on, get out of here!" the Police Dogs barked, encouraging their sniffer-humans to enter the doorway and flush them out. The frightened human refugees staggered to their feet and continued on their weary journey. To where? A family of humans, a mother and father and two small sobbing child-humans, with nowhere to go, nothing to look forward to, chased down the street by ferocious sniffer-humans.

What can those sniffer-humans be
feeling, thought Becky? Forced to be
cruel to their own kind. Maybe their
Police Dog owners train them not to
feel. It can't be right, she thought, as
the human family hobbled away. It
can't be right.

She passed old Mrs Mole being
carefully led to the shops by her guide-
human. Mrs Mole was blind. Her
guide-human was her best friend and

kept her safe. So humans could be useful, thought Becky.

And fun, too. She remembered her birthday party when the Great Rabbito entertained with magic tricks. He showed his hat empty, waved his magic wand, said the magic word, 'Abracadabra', and out popped a cuddly baby-human! A happy baby-human who had made her laugh. Like those humans at the zoo. They had a Humans' Tea Party, and the little human sploshed custard in the big human's face. Great fun. But now, Becky was beginning to wonder whether it was really fair to make humans perform like that.

She thought of Norman. The Bears loved their pet-human. She was sure he loved them. Did he care about other humans? Had he been upset by those television reports? Becky hoped he had slept through them.

She arrived at the school gate and crossed the playground.

"Hi, Becky," called out her friends, Chas Chimp, Freda Ferret and Patch Badger. "Come and play."

But Becky walked on, her mind too full of serious things to join in playground games.

In the history lesson later that day Miss Emu, Becky's teacher, explained the Rise and Fall of the Human Empire. It seems that long, long ago human beings ruled the world, but made a terrible mess of it. They kept having wars and killing each other. And the cleverer they became, inventing things and trying to make a better world, the more they polluted the Earth and changed the balance of Nature. The weather got too hot for them. The seas rose and many drowned. Crops wouldn't grow and humans starved. They nearly succeeded in killing themselves off completely. And, with so few humans left, it was natural that other creatures should take over. The Animal Kingdom now ruled the world.

The remaining humans had to

survive in the more sensible world of the animals. A few, like Mrs Mole's guide-human, and like the sniffer-humans used by the Police Dogs, were useful to animals. Some, like the Great Rabbito's cuddly baby-human and circus performers, worked as entertainers. A lucky few were pets, like Norman. Not-so-lucky ones provided sport for animals of leisure. Fishing, Big Human Hunting, Human-racing and so on. Some were specially bred for food.

But, Miss Emu concluded, on the whole human beings had little real use any more and their numbers would probably dwindle over the coming years, until eventually they would become extinct like their predecessors the Dinosaurs and the Dodos. Mum was right, thought Becky.

That night Becky Bear lay in bed cuddling her favourite doll. She could hear her mother reading Ben a bedtime story. It was the one about a family of humans all dressed up like animals who go on holiday to the seaside. Ben loved that story. And Becky remembered loving it when she was his age. As she dozed off to sleep, she wondered why it was that young animals so loved stories about humans, but cared so little for them when they grew older.

Chapter 3

"COME ON, NORMAN. Walkies!"

Norman happily answered Becky
Bear's call. He fetched his lead and
waited for her to slip it gently round
his neck.

Mrs Bear's voice called from the
kitchen. "Can Ben come too?"

"Of course," replied Becky.

Pushing Ben in his bear-buggy and
with Norman following, she set off for
the park. It was the weekend, so there
was no school. Becky often took

17

Norman and Ben for a walk at the weekend.

As they entered the park gates, they could see Chas Chimp, Freda Ferret and Patch Badger over by the lake, playing in the sunshine.

"Come on," said Becky. "Let's go and meet them."

Chas and Patch had brought their pet-humans along too. They let them off their leads and started to play ball with them.

"Fetch," cried Chas, throwing the ball to Patch. The pet-humans chased towards Patch, who threw the ball to Freda.

"Fetch," cried Patch. The pet-humans chased towards Freda, who threw the ball to Chas.

"Fetch," she cried. The pet-humans, over-excited by now, chased towards

Chas. One caught the ball. The other tried to snatch it. The first refused to give it up. The other tried harder to grab it. And in no time at all they were fighting for it, rolling on the ground, fists flying. Chas, Patch and Freda gathered round them, enjoying the tussle and egging them on.

"Go on boy, get it!" yelled Chas.

"Quick, grab it! Grab it!" shouted Patch.

"Fight! Fight!" squealed Freda.

Becky, pulling Norman and pushing Ben, hurried to the scene. "Stop them. Stop them at once!" she cried.

Her friends laughed. "Run away, Becky," jeered Chas.

"Get the ball! Get it!" Patch shrieked. But the two pet-humans had forgotten the ball and were just bashing and biffing one another.

19

"Fight, fight!" screamed Freda.

Norman nervously shrank back from the disturbing sight. "It's all right, Norman," Becky reassured him. "I won't let you join in."

Ben started to cry. Becky turned his bear-buggy round to stop him seeing the fight.

But Chas, Patch and Freda were enjoying it. As the pet-humans pummelled and punched each other, they whooped and cheered and jumped up and down with excitement.

Becky pushed her way back to the fray. "Stop them, please," she begged. "It's not fair, teasing them like that."

"Come off it, Becky," said Chas. "It's only a bit of fun."

"Not for the humans, it's not," cried Becky.

"Don't interfere, Becky," said

Freda. "They enjoy fighting anyway."

"That's no reason to encourage them," countered Becky angrily. "It's cruelty to dumb humans, don't you see that?"

Suddenly a high-pitched scream rent the air. The animals swung round.

"Becky, look!" shouted Chas.

Becky looked in horror as the bear-buggy rolled down the steep bank towards the lake. Ben, his little arms flailing helplessly, screamed as the bear-buggy picked up speed and splashed into the edge of the lake. Then it hit a large pebble and threw Ben out into the deep muddy water.

Everyone dashed to the water's edge, then hesitated. "I can't swim," gasped Becky.

"Nor can we," cried the others. They hated water.

"Help! Help!" yelled Ben.

Suddenly Norman strode to the lake, waded in and swam strongly towards the floundering Ben. Bravely he took him in his arms, and, keeping his head above water, carried him safely back to shore.

Everyone cheered. "Thank you, Norman," cried Becky.

"Good boy," said Chas.

"Brave Norman," smiled Freda.

Norman smiled happily and handed

Ben safely to Becky, proud to have saved his little master.

"You're a hero," said Patch.

But the other pet-humans didn't think Norman was a hero. Limping and bruised from their fight, they sidled up to him and eyed him with scorn. Animal-lover, they seemed to say. Dirty animal-lover. They went to hit him, but thought better of it and slunk back to their owners.

Chas, Patch and Freda said goodbye and set off, feeling rather guilty. They knew that the accident might not have happened if they hadn't been teasing their pet-humans.

When Ben had calmed down and dried out a little, Becky started to push him home. Norman followed modestly behind. They left the park and crossed the road.

Suddenly a large van screeched to a halt beside them. Out jumped two vast Securiboars in uniform, their trotters wielding truncheons. Becky knew Securiboars meant trouble. She assumed they were looking for human refugees. But, grunting and snorting, gnashing their sharp tusks, they advanced and roughly pushed Becky and Ben to one side. Then they grabbed Norman and bundled him into the back of the van.

"No, please!" cried Becky.

But it was too late. The doors slammed in her face, and the Securiboars' van drove off at speed and disappeared round the corner.

Chapter 4

HER HEAD IN a whirl and fighting back the tears, Becky dashed home, giving Ben such an exciting ride in his bear-buggy he almost forgot Norman was not with them.

"What on earth's the matter?" cried Mrs Bear.

"Oh, Mum," said Becky, and breathlessly explained what had happened.

Mr Bear interrupted his gardening to listen too.

"Poor Norman," said Mrs Bear quietly. "He saved Ben, and then . . ."

"If only I could have saved *him*," wailed Becky.

"Where *is* Norman?" whispered Ben, not really understanding what had happened.

"Oh, Ben," said Mrs Bear, giving him a hug.

"Will we ever see him again, Dad?" asked Becky.

Mr Bear puffed thoughtfully on his pipe. "You've told us about the Securiboars," he started.

"Two of them," blurted Becky. "In a big van. It all happened so quickly. They just took him."

"Yes, I know," nodded her father patiently. "But what colour was the van? Try to remember."

"Red," replied Becky. She gasped.

"I've just thought. It had letters written on the side. A word. I know, H.A.R.M."

Mr Bear's pipe nearly fell out of his mouth. "H.A.R.M?" he repeated softly. Becky nodded.

"Then I'm afraid, my girl, we may have lost dear old Norman for good."

Mrs Bear looked up from comforting Ben.

"You see, Becky," said Mr Bear. "The letters H.A.R.M. stand for Human Analysis and Research Ministry."

"Never heard of it," said Chas Chimp.

"Human Analysis and Research Ministry," Becky Bear repeated. "It's a place where they do tests and things on humans. Scientists trying out new medicines. Antibiotics, that kind of thing. They experiment on humans."

The friends were standing in a corner of the school playground during break the following Monday.

"They couldn't give new medicines to us animals without testing them first," said Patch Badger. "Stands to reason."

"But why test them on poor Norman?" spluttered Becky. "It's not fair."

"Especially after he saved your little brother," said Freda Ferret thoughtfully.

"Exactly," said Becky. "Norman's one of the family. He's not just a human. He's an honorary animal."

"I can't see there's much you can do, my old mate," sighed Chas Chimp. The bell rang. "Hey up, back to the grindstone."

"Listen," said Becky, as they all headed for the classroom. "After school. Will you help? I've got a plan."

The Human Analysis and Research Ministry was a dark, unwelcoming building surrounded by a high wall crowned with barbed wire.

After school, Becky Bear and her friends nervously approached the gatehouse.

"What do you lot want?" snorted an unfriendly voice. The huge, bristly head of a Securiboar leered down at them. "You're not thinking of trespassing, are you? 'Cos if you are, I might be thinking of persecution."

"Don't you mean prosecution?" enquired Chas Chimp cheekily.

"Both if necessary," snorted the Securiboar.

Becky hastily changed the subject. "Sorry to bother you, sir," she smiled politely, "but we're doing a project at school. All about health and research into disease, that sort of thing . . ."

"Well?"

"Well, our teacher suggested we might interview the Director of this Ministry."

"Get some facts and figures," added Freda Ferret.

"Straight from the horse's mouth," chipped in Chas.

The Securiboar stiffened. "The Director's not a horse," he snorted. "You want to get your facts right."

"Exactly, sir," said Becky quickly. "That's why we've come here."

After a pause, the Securiboar told them to hang on a minute. Pulling a portable telephone from his jacket pocket, he pressed some of the buttons and waited. Suddenly he stood stiffly to attention.

"Hallo. Director, sir? Security here, sir. Group of school animals want to view you."

"*Inter*view, stupid," hissed Chas. Becky hurriedly shushed him.

"Watch it!" snorted the Securiboar, covering the telephone and glaring at Chas. Then, uncovering the telephone, "Interview you, sir. For a reject."

"*Pro*ject, dummy," said Patch Badger rudely. Becky shushed him.

"Watch it!" snorted the Securiboar, glaring at Patch but forgetting to cover the telephone. "Oh, no sir, not you, sir, sorry sir." His bristly face blushed. "For a project." He paused for an answer. The friends looked nervously at each other.

"Right, sir. Very good, sir." He coughed and stuffed the telephone back in his pocket.

"The Director has agreed to receive you," he grunted reluctantly. "First left. Across the courtyard. In the main entrance."

"Oh, thank you," said Becky as the friends set off.

"Wait for it," snorted the Securiboar. The friends stopped. He eyed them suspiciously and shook a warning trotter. "Watch it!"

As they crossed the courtyard to the main entrance, the friends smiled and winked at each other. Becky's plan was working. The Securiboar hadn't told the Director exactly how many school animals to expect.

The Director's office was just inside the main entrance. The four friends prepared to knock on the door. But only three friends prepared to enter. Becky, checking the coast was clear, set off down a long, forbidding corridor. The others waved and whispered good luck. Then Chas plucked up the courage to knock.

"Enter," boomed a terrifying voice. The door opened and Chas, Patch and Freda found themselves in the awesome presence of Professor Rhino.

Chapter 5

NORMAN AWOKE. HE tried to work out where he was. In the dim light he stretched out his hands and touched a cold metallic wall. He felt along it, found a corner, then another wall, another corner, another wall and then a number of vertical bars. He shook the bars. They rattled but hardly moved. Norman tried to stand, but hit his head on the low ceiling. He was locked in a cage, and as he sank to the floor he found himself sitting on straw that was damp and dirty.

34

He remembered being captured by two rough animals. He remembered being bundled into the back of a van. He remembered a sharp stinging pain as something was jabbed into his arm. But after that, his mind was a blank.

Suddenly he heard a sound. An urgent tapping sound. From the cage next door. Pressing his face tight to the bars, Norman could just see two frightened eyes staring into his. A female human face, forlorn and nervous as Norman's. A flicker of a smile, a flash of hope at finding a fellow victim. Norman stretched a hand through the bars. The female human did the same. Her hand found Norman's. He held it.

Tiptoeing warily down the corridor, Becky Bear passed doors marked

Doctor Beagle, *Sister Guinea-pig* and
Professor Rhesus. But there was no sign
of the place where she feared Norman
might be – the H.A.R.M. laboratory.

Suddenly, she heard voices. Two
white rats in nurses' uniform rounded
the corner ahead and scurried towards
her. Becky threw herself through an
open door into a store cupboard. The
rat-nurses passed by.

Becky waited till their footsteps
faded, then gingerly crept back into the
corridor. Rounding the corner she
headed in the direction the rat-nurses
had come from.

A few steps further and there it was!
A door marked *Laboratory*. *Private*.
Ministry Personnel Only. Becky pushed
the door. It swung open. She entered a
long room lined with hundreds of
cages. In each cage huddled a human.

Some appeared to be asleep. Some had tubes and wires attached to them. Some looked terrified as Becky, making her way down the line, peered into each cage. "I'm not going to hurt you," she whispered.

Becky reached the end of the room, then started to return along the opposite wall. About twenty cages down her heart skipped a beat. There he was! Norman! Eyes closed. But still breathing. Asleep.

The cage was not padlocked, but bolted from the outside. Becky carefully slid the bolt and started to open the door. Then she noticed Norman's hand, gripped tightly by a hand from the cage next door. The female human it belonged to gazed imploringly at Becky. Becky tried to ignore her.

"Norman!" she called gently.

Norman woke. He saw Becky and smiled thankfully. Again Becky tried to open the door, but the clasped hands stopped her.

"Come along, Norman," she

38

whispered. "We're going home."

Tears welled in Norman's eyes. He looked towards his young mistress, then towards his new friend, then back again.

Becky understood. She slid back the bolt on the other cage. The two humans released their grip and both doors swung open. The two humans clambered out, hugged each other, then looked gratefully at Becky, who hurried them towards the exit.

As they left, hundreds of arms pressed through the bars of hundreds of cages as hundreds of humans, hands outstretched, begged to be saved too.

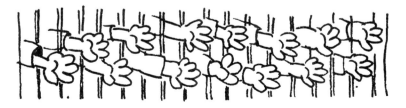

Chapter 6

PROFESSOR RHINO WAS flattered to have such an attentive young audience. At first, Chas, Patch and Freda had been nervous of the enormous white-coated figure looming over them, but they had managed to explain the purpose of their visit with just the right amount of shyness and respect to encourage the Professor to relax. He welcomed them, and, peering at them from behind his huge desk, described to them the work of the Ministry.

40

"Have any of you ever suffered from ringworm?" he enquired. "Rabies? Foot and mouth disease? Scurvy? Distemper? Myxomatosis?"

The friends shuddered and shook their heads.

"No sir," whispered Freda.

"Of course not!" Professor Rhino exclaimed triumphantly. "I and my colleagues have thoroughly researched these diseases and wiped them from the face of the earth. Impressive, eh?"

The friends nodded approvingly and took notes. But secretly they wondered how many humans had been forced to suffer in the cause of the Ministry's work, and if poor Norman had already become Professor Rhino's latest victim.

"We quite understand, sir," said Patch, "that some experiments are necessary on humans, but . . ."

"Indeed they are!" interrupted Professor Rhino. "If we animal scientists were to experiment on other animals, just imagine the howls of protest we would receive from the general animal public!"

"But do the humans suffer much pain?" asked Freda.

"Of course not," smiled the Professor reassuringly. "Our scientists are trained to damage them as little as possible. We value them too much. You see . . ." he lowered his voice, "the fact is humans are becoming rather scarce. Quite difficult to come by."

"Is that why you send out vans looking for them?" asked Chas.

"We saw one the other day," added Patch.

"Really? Most observant of you,"

said Professor Rhino carefully. "Yes, we are allowed to pick up, er . . . stray humans wandering the streets."

"But not pet-humans?" said Freda innocently.

"Pet-humans?" Professor Rhino laughed loudly. "Of course not, my dear. Of course not."

The friends looked at each other. And then the alarm bell rang.

Professor Rhino's eyes bulged. He sprang from his chair. "Excuse me. Emergency!" he muttered, and charged headlong from the office.

"Nurse Rat!" he roared down the corridor. "What's going on?"

"An escape, Professor, an escape!" came the panic-stricken reply. The Professor lumbered down the corridor, leaving Chas, Patch and Freda nervously peeping round the office door.

The alarm bell rang and rang. Becky, Norman and Norman's friend had just escaped from the laboratory when they heard it. They threw themselves into an empty office and hid behind a desk. They were just in time. Doors opened and footsteps echoed through the Ministry as doctors, nurses and Securiboars hurtled along the corridor towards the laboratory.

When all seemed quiet, Becky checked that the coast was clear and started to lead the pet-humans back into the corridor. Suddenly she spotted a file marked *Top Secret* lying on the desk. Taking a deep breath, knowing she was committing a crime, Becky took it.

Down the corridor they raced till they met up with Chas, Patch and Freda by the Director's office. Then, leaving the main H.A.R.M. building, they crept carefully round the gatehouse. From inside they heard the

Securiboar squealing down his portable telephone. "No sir, no sir. I haven't seen a single animal come out, sir. No sir, really, sir, I wasn't asleep on duty, sir, believe me, sir . . ."

His voice faded as Becky and her friends picked up speed and raced through the dark streets towards home.

Mr and Mrs Bear were waiting anxiously.

"Where have you been, Becky?" cried Mrs Bear. "You're very late."

"I'm fine Mum, really," said Becky.

"We were worried," grunted Mr Bear.

But when they saw Norman, the Bears were overjoyed and asked no further questions. They even welcomed Norman's friend, who clung nervously to Norman, her big eyes imploring the

Bear family to let her stay. They decided to call her Norma, and opened two tins of tasty human-food for the hungry pets, who tucked in gratefully. Norman insisted on offering Norma his basket, and Mrs Bear found him an old blanket to lie on. Before long, still tightly holding hands, they fell fast asleep.

Mr Bear turned on the television for the late-night news.

"Good evening, good evening!" announced Newshound. "Here is the latest update. Two humans escaped from the Human Analysis and Research Ministry tonight."

Mrs Bear looked up in alarm.

Newshound continued. "It is thought this daring escape was planned and carried out by a group of school animals. Professor Rhino, the

Ministry's director, has ordered a Securiboar search of the surrounding streets. Here ends this update."

"Oh Becky, you didn't," said Mrs Bear quietly.

"I had to, Mum," said Becky.

Mr Bear frowned. "We'll have to keep Norman and Norma indoors for a while," he said. "During the day, anyway. Maybe take them for walks at night, when it's dark. Those Securiboars mean business."

Chapter 7

THAT NIGHT, BECKY lay in bed trying to
sleep. But every time she closed her
eyes moving pictures filled her head.
She saw Norman and Norma running,
frightened. Two Securiboars,
truncheons raised, chased after them.
She saw a family of refugee-humans
desperately searching the streets for
somewhere, anywhere to live. Police
dogs with sniffer-humans waited round
every corner, allowing them no rest,
flushing them from the shelter of shop

doorways and forcing them to move on, on, on.

In her mind, Becky saw again the television pictures of hundreds of refugee-humans being ordered out of their tower blocks. In terror they fled towards her. They seemed to advance further and further until they burst from the television screen, screaming to Becky, "Help, help!"

Then suddenly she was back in the laboratory at H.A.R.M. She saw rows and rows of cages, all with humans trapped inside, staring at her, hands outstretched, begging her to free them. Please, Becky, please, said the expressions on their sad faces, help us, help us.

After school dinner next day, Becky and her friends met as usual in the playground.

"Thanks for yesterday," said Becky. "You were all brilliant."

"Our pleasure," smiled Chas Chimp.

"We enjoyed it," said Freda Ferret.

"It was exciting," agreed Patch. "How's Norman?"

"He's fine," said Becky. "And his friend. We've called her Norma." She beckoned them into a huddle. "Now, everyone," she announced importantly. "Look at this."

Carefully Becky showed them the file marked *Top Secret*. "I found it in an office at H.A.R.M."

"A bit dangerous, stealing it," said Patch quietly.

"Maybe," said Becky. "But just as well I did." She opened the file. "Listen." She read a typed document. "Confidential memo. Because of the growing worldwide shortage of humans, a regular supply for experimental research is becoming harder to obtain. From now on, all Securiboars have the power to arrest or capture not just strays but *all* humans they can find. Signed Professor Rhino, Director."

"So he was lying to us yesterday," gasped Freda.

"Of course," said Becky. "And don't you see? The more tower blocks they demolish, the more humans become homeless, and the more likely they are to end up in H.A.R.M."

"They'll soon be extinct anyway," said Chas. "We learned that in history."

Patch nodded. "There's nothing anyone can do, I reckon."

"But there must be," cried Becky. "And we're the animals to do it. We've got to tell the world to save the humans before it's too late."

"Save the humans?" Patch blinked. "Us?"

"Why not?" yelled Becky, her eyes shining. "A campaign! SAVE THE HUMAN. Are you with me?"

The campaign started with a petition. Becky and her friends invited all the animals at their school and their parents to sign. The results were encouraging. Many animals, especially the younger ones, wanted to save the human. Some of the older ones still didn't see the point of it. The world, they thought, was fine as it was. Why stop the human becoming extinct? Who needed more humans?

54

Becky began to raise money. With Chas, Patch and Freda she organised an animobile boot sale where they sold their old toys, and she persuaded the Head of the school to donate the ticket-money from the school play, *The Taming of the Shrew*, to the campaign fund. Soon there was enough money to make SAVE THE HUMAN badges. These raised even more money, enough to print thousands of leaflets explaining the aims of SAVE THE HUMAN. The Pigeon Post Office Union kindly agreed that its members should deliver the leaflets free, and soon animals far and wide were writing to Becky, joining the campaign, and organising special fund-raising events. Pigs held sponsored slims. In Africa the animals held jungle sales and the Buffaloes enjoyed a Fun Stampede. The

Kangaroos of Australia ran sponsored hops and in the oceans of the world thousands of sea creatures took part in sponsored swims.

A mammoth march took place when animals of every size and shape carried banners proclaiming SAVE THE HUMAN NOW, and ACT WHILE THERE'S TIME, and JUSTICE FOR DEFENCELESS HUMANS. Now many older animals got caught up in the growing enthusiasm. They were impressed by Becky's sincerity and opened their minds to the plight of humans. More and more began to understand and, to show their support, joined the campaign.

As leader of the campaign Becky Bear became its spokesanimal. Mr and Mrs Bear proudly watched her being interviewed on television.

"Tell us, Becky," said Newshound, "what's the latest update on SAVE THE HUMAN?"

"I am proud to announce," declared Becky, "our first Annual Conference, to be attended by delegates from all corners of the globe, creatures of the earth, the sky and the sea. After democratic debate, we will publish the SAVE THE HUMAN manifesto and force the governments of the world to unite and take action. SAVE THE HUMAN!"

The Conference was held at the seaside, so that every creature could attend.

"The human should be a protected species," declared the Dolphins.

"No more hunting humans for sport," roared the Tigers.

57

"Fattening up humans for food must stop!" cackled the Geese.

"Hunting humans for their skins should be a crime," snapped the Crocodiles.

"Save the human habitat," screeched the Apes.

"Close the zoos and create special Wild Human Estates," growled the Polar Bears.

"Give humans back their dignity," trumpeted the Elephants. "No more circuses!"

"Ban all research experiments on humans," cried Becky Bear, cheered on by Chas, Patch and Freda.

"Hear, hear!" cheered every delegate. "Hear, hear!"

The Human Aid concert was Becky's greatest triumph. The largest television audience ever! Featuring every famous rock band from the Funky Monkies to the Beetles! In the royal presence of the Prince and Princess of Whales!

"Creatures of the world," yelled the DJ into the microphone. "A big, big welcome to the greatest, grooviest rock concert in the Earth's history!"

Thousands of animals packed into the huge arena cheered.

"Featuring all your favourite, fabulous artistes live by TV satellite to every corner of the globe! It's Human Aid!"

The applause was deafening.

"And who dreamed the whole thing up?" cried the DJ. "Our own, one and only, Becky Bear!"

The crowd roared as Becky, nervous but thrilled, stepped into the spotlight

at the front of the stage. The DJ
handed her the microphone.

"Thank you, thank you," she said
modestly. "And now it's time to meet
the Kings of the Jungle sound – the
Pride!"

The crowd went wild as four lions
entered and performed their latest hit,
'Rock 'n' Roar'. Lights flashed, the
audience joined in, and on a huge
screen behind the band the words

SAVE THE HUMAN encouraged creatures worldwide to donate money to the campaign.

The concert lasted eight hours, and at regular intervals Becky appealed to the television audience. "Please, please support us. SAVE THE HUMAN!"

The money poured in. The animal public became aware of the humans' plight. The world's press proclaimed the news. 'Human Aid Rocks The World', 'Becky Bear Megastar', 'Human Aid Raises Fortune For SAVE THE HUMAN', ran the headlines.

Soon the governments of the world were forced to take notice. A special meeting of world leaders was called. And Becky Bear was invited to address the United Creations. It was her proudest moment. In the presence of the world's most powerful political figures she stood alone on the platform and made her speech.

"Friends. You, world leaders all, have the power. I, a humble schoolbear, have the will. You are just. I seek justice. You are wise. I seek wisdom. Friends, I humbly and heartily beg you to get your act together and Save the Human *now*!"

After a pause, the assembly burst into spontaneous, heartfelt applause. They voted unanimously to help Becky and her campaign.

At home Norman and Norma watched their caring young mistress on Mr and Mrs Bear's television. They smiled.

In his office at H.A.R.M. Professor Rhino was also watching Becky on television. He was not smiling.

Chapter 8

SLOWLY BUT SURELY things began to
improve. The human became a
protected species. Hunting humans for
sport, food or their skins became a
thing of the past.

Humans were allowed to keep their
tower blocks, and splendid Wild
Human Estates were created, showing
humans living in specially designed
recreations of their own habitat.
Animals in families and school parties
flocked to see them, and enjoyed

learning about these creatures, whom they now accepted had a right to share the earth with them. Some animals joined "Adopt-a-human" schemes and many stray humans were rescued and given good homes. And, as the world became a safer place for humans, so their numbers began to increase.

In his office at H.A.R.M., Professor Rhino summoned his staff to a meeting.

"I have been informed," he announced, "by Sir Reynard Fox, the Minister for the Environment, that from now on all experimental testing on humans is illegal."

His scientists, doctors and nurses gasped.

"Our jobs are at risk," the Professor continued. "Our life's work is at risk.

Thanks to Becky Bear's stupid campaign, humans are a protected species and we can no longer use them for our research. And without our research we can no longer prevent the spread of sickness and disease throughout the animal kingdom. Our work is essential for public animal health. It must continue!"

His staff nodded. Professor Rhino peered at his team of ruthless Securiboars. "We need humans," he snarled. "Go find us humans. Now!"

That night H.A.R.M. vans stealthily roamed the streets in search of humans. Suddenly they would screech to a halt and two Securiboars, snorting and grunting, would clamber out and grab an unsuspecting human enjoying an evening stroll. Pet-humans were dragged from their animal owners.

65

Even humans living on Wild Human Estates were not safe. All were thrown roughly into the vans, which transported them at speed through the night towards H.A.R.M. and Professor Rhino's waiting cages. Soon the laboratory was full, and the Professor's eager staff were preparing to recommence their experiments.

After school dinner next day, Chas, Patch and Freda stood silently in the playground. Suddenly Freda spotted Becky walking thoughtfully towards the gate.

"Hi, Becky!" she called.

Becky turned. "Hallo, Freda," she said. "Can't stop. Got a meeting."

Freda's face fell. "Another meeting?" she said. Becky was always going to meetings these days.

"About the new Centre for Human Studies. I've got the afternoon off school," Becky told her. "What's the matter with them?" she asked, seeing Chas and Patch's miserable faces.

Freda sighed. "The Securiboars snatched their pet-humans yesterday," she said.

"Oh," said Becky. "I'm sorry."

"H.A.R.M. should be closed down," said Chas.

"No chance, I'm afraid," replied Becky. "Not yet anyway. I had a meeting with Professor Rhino."

This was news to the others. They looked up. "What did he say?" asked Patch.

"Nothing new. He believes his work benefits all animal life. I suppose we have to respect that."

"Nonsense," cried Freda. "You don't really believe that. If you do, why did you rescue Norman?"

"That was different," Becky explained patiently. "He was my pet."

"What's so special about *your* pet?" argued Chas. "Why aren't we rescuing other people's pets?"

"*Our* pets," said Patch.

"And all the other wretched humans

suffering under Rhino?" cried Chas.

"Hear, hear!" chanted the others.

"Come on, Becky," said Freda. "We helped you. Please help us."

"I'm sorry," said Becky quietly. "SAVE THE HUMAN has never committed crimes to plead its cause. Peaceful persuasion is still the right way. Believe me."

But the friends didn't believe her. Becky's changed, they thought. And as she set off for her meeting, they secretly made plans which didn't involve her. They decided to go it alone.

Late that evening, three animals wearing hoods crept towards the H.A.R.M. gatehouse. Suddenly the Securiboar on duty spotted them. Snorting furiously he grabbed Freda

and raised his truncheon. Freda
screamed. Chas rushed to the rescue.
Bravely he struggled to pull Freda free.
The Securiboar dropped his truncheon
and lunged at Chas, pinioning his
arms behind his back. Patch,
panicking, picked up the truncheon
and bopped the Securiboar on the
head. He didn't like violence, but he
had to rescue his friends. The
Securiboar dropped to the ground,
semi-conscious.

70

Chas, Patch and Freda made their escape. They sped to the main entrance, passed the Director's office door, and carefully made their way down the dimly-lit corridor.

They reached the laboratory. Suddenly the door opened. Chas, Patch and Freda flung themselves behind it as Dr Beagle and Nurse Rat emerged and set off down the corridor.

Chas peeped round the door. All was clear. He beckoned the others, and led them gingerly inside the laboratory.

Each cage contained a frightened human. Chas, Patch and Freda peered in every one till they found, to their excitement, Chas and Patch's pet-humans. Carefully they unbolted the cages and helped their grateful pets escape.

Immediately the other imprisoned humans stretched their hands through the bars, appealing to be saved too. Chas, Patch and Freda looked at each other and nodded. Soon every single cage was open.

"Go on! Run!" they hissed to the stunned inmates. "You're free!"

Hundreds of humans raced out into the night and joyfully drank in the cool fresh air.

Freda with Chas and Patch and their pet-humans escaped to their homes, proud of their action. They had SAVED THE HUMAN, and how!

The Securiboar, head bandaged, stood nervously in the Director's office. "You fool," raged Professor Rhino. "You incompetent fool!"

"Yes sir, sorry sir," snuffled the

Securiboar. "They were too quick for me, sir."

"My life's work ruined!" wailed Professor Rhino. "Not one research human left! Hundreds lost! Hundreds! Who did it? Who?"

"Don't ask me, sir. They had their faces covered. But look, sir. One of them dropped this in the lab." He held out a badge.

Professor Rhino grabbed it. "I might have guessed!" he roared. "SAVE THE HUMAN! It's that Bear! That meddling little Bear!"

Chapter 9

ALL THIS TIME, Becky had been at home, in bed asleep. Next morning, when the Bear family gathered for breakfast, she turned on the television as usual.

"Good day, good day!" announced Newshound. "Here is the latest update."

"I want a drink, please," said little Ben.

"Quiet, Ben," snapped his mother.

"I said please," complained Ben.

74

"Shhh," hissed his father.

"News is coming in," barked Newshound, "of a mass escape of research humans from the laboratory of H.A.R.M."

Becky looked up from her toast and honey.

"It is suspected that members of the SAVE THE HUMAN campaign were responsible," announced Newshound.

"Oh no," cried Becky. "Chas, Patch and Freda. I tried to warn them."

Suddenly there was a loud knocking on the door followed by the sound of a rough voice. "Open up, open up!" it bellowed.

"What on earth. . . ?" started Mrs Bear.

Two Securiboars hurtled into the room. One seized Becky. The other guarded the door.

"You're coming with us," grunted the first. "Professor Rhino's orders. Subversive suspicion. I mean, suspective subvection. Or something like that."

Mrs Bear intervened. "You can't take my daughter," she shouted. "It was nothing to do with her."

"We're not taking your daughter," snorted the second Securiboar, lumbering forward and grabbing Mrs Bear. "We're taking all of you."

He wrenched Ben from his high chair, and, protesting loudly but to no avail, the Bear family was herded outside.

Norman, who had been asleep under the table, awoke, and watched in horror as his caring owners were bundled into the Securiboar's van, the very van in which he had been captured before. Norma joined him at the window. She owed her life to the Bears. As she watched them driven away, she wondered if she and Norman would ever see them again.

In the H.A.R.M. laboratory, the vast shape of Professor Rhino loomed threateningly over a row of adjoining cages, into which the Securiboars had bolted the Bear family.

"Mummy!" screamed Ben.

From the next cage Mrs Bear extended a paw and squeezed one of Ben's.

"Aha," sneered Professor Rhino. "The SAVE THE HUMAN mob. Welcome!"

"Listen," called Mr Bear, "you can't treat us like this. How dare you!"

The Professor's neck stiffened and

his eyes bulged. "How dare your wretched daughter ruin my life's work!" he snarled. "Without humans to test on, how can I make the world a better place?"

"I want to make the world a better place too," shouted Becky defiantly.

"In that case," said Professor Rhino, calmly and coldly, "I'm quite sure you will not mind sacrificing your family and yourself to the cause of my animal welfare research. Tomorrow," he chuckled, "we will commence experiments. On you!"

Chapter 10

CHAS, PATCH AND Freda had set free the research humans thinking they would be happy, thinking they would be grateful.

But many of them felt nothing but anger with the animal kingdom for having locked them up in H.A.R.M. in the first place. Now, in their hundreds, they roamed the city in packs, determined on and thirsting for revenge. They rampaged through the streets, smashing windows and breaking into animals' homes. They destroyed property, set fire to buildings and terrified innocent animals.

News of the human riots spread. Other humans decided to join the rebels. Pet-humans attacked their animal owners, performing humans refused to perform, working humans stopped working and joined their colleagues on the streets.

They stormed the Wild Human Estates, encouraging the humans who lived there to revolt. Chaos reigned. The animals pleaded with the humans to stop. But to no avail. The humans were merciless in their lust for revenge.

Norman and Norma sadly watched the crisis develop on the Bears' television.

"Update! Update!" barked Newshound. "Following the mysterious disappearance of their leader, Becky Bear, SAVE THE HUMAN announce a Crisis Conference at the seaside. The world is in chaos! Animals are dying! Is history repeating itself? Will humans take over the world?"

Chas, Patch and Freda could hardly believe the disastrous results of their actions. Both Chas and Patch's pet-humans, having been saved from H.A.R.M. by their young owners, turned against them and joined the animals in the streets.

The news of the Bear family's disappearance made the three friends feel even worse. Not wanting to let Becky down further, they set off for the Crisis Conference at the seaside.

The behaviour of their fellow humans filled Norman and Norma with shame.

Surely this wasn't what Becky, their young mistress, had intended. Fairness for humans was one thing, but humans fighting animals to take over the world was another. Norman and Norma loved their animal owners. Now they had a new mission. To SAVE THE BEARS.

In the dead of night, they left the house and gingerly made their way through the rubble of burnt-out houses

and gangs of looting hooligan-humans roaming the streets, looking for trouble.

They arrived outside H.A.R.M. They crept past a snoring Securiboar in the gatehouse, passed through the main entrance and ran down the deserted corridor towards the laboratory.

The Bears were overjoyed to see their pet-humans. Norman and Norma slid back the bolts, opened the cage doors, and greeted their owners with tears of happiness. Then they started to lead the Bears towards the laboratory door. Suddenly heavy footsteps echoed from the corridor outside. Quickly Norman and Norma ushered the Bears into a cage near the door. Immediately the door opened and Professor Rhino, carrying a hypodermic syringe full of his latest experimental vaccine, eagerly headed for the cages in which he had bolted his victims. He stopped. His eyes bulged in bewilderment. The cage doors were swinging ajar. The cages were empty! Mystified he slowly lumbered inside one to check. The Bears must be here, he thought. Escape is impossible. As he groped around inside, Norman and Norma raced up to the cage, slammed the door shut, and firmly slid the bolt into place.

Professor Rhino roared and ranted, but it was too late. He was well and truly locked inside. As he sank to the floor in helpless fury he felt a jab penetrate the thick hide of his rear. "No! No!" he raved in terrified disbelief. "I have injected myself!"

Norman and Norma rushed back to

the Bears and led them to safety, just as Becky had rescued *them*.

With great care they guided the Bears through war-torn streets where animal-hating humans lurked, ready to attack. For several days and nights they travelled, refugees from violence and intolerance.

At last they reached the seaside.

The SAVE THE HUMAN Crisis Conference was due to start, but no animals had arrived to take part. Many would not risk the journey. And, in the light of recent developments, many no longer felt able to support the campaign.

"It's all over," said Becky quietly.

Her father comforted her. "You tried, Becky. You did your best."

"And we're safe," said her mother.

Chas, Patch and Freda arrived.

Becky welcomed them with a tired
smile.

"You made it then!" cried Patch.

Becky nodded.

"And so did we!" said Freda.

"But nobody else," sighed Becky.

"It was our fault," said Chas.
"We're sorry, Becky."

"No, it was my fault," said Becky.
"I got big-headed. Carried away.

Forgot who my real friends are. I'm the one who's sorry!"

"But we should never have broken into H.A.R.M. and saved those humans," said Patch. "That's what started it."

Becky looked thoughtful. "Maybe we should never have started it in the first place," she said slowly. "Maybe the humans weren't ready to be saved. Maybe they shouldn't have any freedom. Maybe they'll make a mess of things like they did last time. Maybe this time they'll destroy themselves.

Flames lit up the night sky and the distant sounds of war disturbed the calm sea air. Becky, her family, her friends and her pet-humans looked sadly inland towards a world once more in turmoil.

Is it possible, wondered Becky, that

Norman and Norma may soon be the last two humans on earth?

Suddenly she saw a boat on the beach.

"Come on!" she whispered. "It's time to go."

The Bears, Norman and Norma, and Chas, Patch and Freda sailed away, leaving the smoky battleground behind them.

They found an empty desert island, miles from anywhere. Together animals and humans started again. Together animals and humans lived in peace.